ALSO BY CHRISTIAN WIMAN

POETRY

Hammer Is the Prayer: Selected Poems

Once in the West

Every Riven Thing

Hard Night

The Long Home

PROSE

He Held Radical Light: The Art of Faith, the Faith of Art

My Bright Abyss: Meditation of a Modern Believer

Ambition and Survival: Becoming a Poet

TRANSLATION

Stolen Air: Selected Poems of Osip Mandelstam

ANTHOLOGY

*The Open Door: One Hundred Poems,
One Hundred Years of* Poetry Magazine (with Don Share)

Joy: 100 Poems

SURVIVAL IS A STYLE

SURVIVAL IS A STYLE

● ● ●

CHRISTIAN WIMAN

FARRAR, STRAUS AND GIROUX

NEW YORK

Farrar, Straus and Giroux
120 Broadway, New York 10271

The Library of Congress has cataloged the hardcover edition as follows:
Names: Wiman, Christian, 1966– author.
Title: Survival is a style / Christian Wiman.
Description: First edition. | New York : Farrar, Straus and Giroux, 2019. |
    Includes bibliographical references.
Identifiers: LCCN 2019036404 | ISBN 9780374272050 (hardcover)
Subjects: LCGFT: Poetry.
Classification: LCC PS3573.I47843 S87 2019 | DDC 811/.54—dc23
LC record available at https://lccn.loc.gov/2019036404

Paperback ISBN: 978-0-374-53933-7

Designed by Gretchen Achilles

Our books may be purchased in bulk for promotional, educational,
or business use. Please contact your local bookseller or the Macmillan
Corporate and Premium Sales Department at 1-800-221-7945, extension 5442,
or by email at MacmillanSpecialMarkets@macmillan.com.

www.fsgbooks.com
www.twitter.com/fsgbooks • www.facebook.com/fsgbooks

3   5   7   9   10   8   6   4   2

For D.

CONTENTS

II

III

IV

SURVIVAL IS A STYLE

PROLOGUE

Church or sermon, prayer or poem:
the failure of religious feeling is a form.

·

The failure of religious feeling is a form
of love that, though it could not survive

the cataclysmic joy of its inception,
nevertheless preserves its own sane something,

a space in which the grievers gather,
inviolate ice that the believers weather:

church or sermon, prayer or poem.

·

Finer and finer the meaningless distinctions:
theodicies, idiolects, books, books, books.

I need a space for unbelief to breathe.
I need a form for failure, since it is what I have.

I

SURVIVAL IS A STYLE

There are no knives
on the man so thin the wind
whips his cargo pants around him like a dance
to which his bones aspire,

no flares, no smoke, no unmetaphorical fire
when the woman in the camouflage jog bra
jogs by whistling all the while.
Survival is a style.

TO EAT THE AWFUL WHILE YOU STARVE YOUR AWE

To eat the awful while you starve your awe,
to weasel misery like a suck of egg,
to be ebullience's prick and leak,
a character pinched to characteristic,
hell-relisher, persimmon-sipper, sad Tom, sane Tom,
all day licking the cicatrix where your Tomhood lay.

DRIVE, 1982

There is no new thing under the sun
but the ever-reviving lives our losses foster,
like the white-bloused girl wading cotton north of Dunn
who looked up the moment that I lost her.

SUMMER RIVER ROSIE DAM

The old bitch Rosie ambles up the drive.
The taut knobs of her teats nearly touch the dust.
Somewhere something needs her.
Chunk-necked, long-bodied, lug-legged, smudge-colored.
She abhors brooms but otherwise endures
insults, indifference, novice efforts to leash or clean.
A kind of commanding obedience about her:
as long as it takes you to see, she waits.
Then, with a sort of conspiratorial shiver and eons in her eyes,
lugs her nubs up the porch steps and sighs loudly down
as if she's been deflated.
A ghost of must and an orbit of fleas,
one toothed ear and two bonus toes.
Nothing culminates in her.
She is the opposite of frolic.
Her sleep is an extinction.
However, should an afternoon prove overlong, heat
smite, one's pleasures pall,
should one let slip the one word she knows
(*Rosie* is a rune to her, one more blurt from the blurters)
she's up! all frisk and ripple, sniffing existence anew,
and with her tail pronged as a warthog saunters
down the steps, across the yard, parting the tall grass ahead of you
toward the roar.

EATING GRAPES DOWNWARD

Every morning without thinking I open
my notebook and see if something
might have grown in me during the night.
Usually, no. But sometimes a tendril
tries a crack in my consciousness
and if I remain only indirectly aware of it
and tether my attention to the imminent
and perhaps ultimately unseeable
sun, sometimes it will grow. Inevitably
a sense of insignificance intrudes: I think
of all the lives in all the places
waiting in their ways
for something to grow out of them,
into them. Is it the same God?

I have a cousin whose political opinions
vile up out of him on the internet
in the most imaginative ways.
He sports a cartoon mustache like Rollie Fingers
that was a lodestone of enduring awe
in my childhood, along with his gift
for scissoring bricks with one blow.
With his spanking *karategi* and cowboy *kiai*,
his weasel-sleek of hair and handlebars,
he was a spectacle there in Midland, Texas,
circa 1973, where the sun slammed
the blacktop and the pumpjacks beaked
the background like prehistoric crows.

Always eat grapes downward,
advises Samuel Butler, a corroded copy
of whose *Notebooks* I perused
at the backwoods Woodbridge bookstore
that seemed, somehow, already erstwhile,
while my daughters fussed and bleated to be
outside with the miniature cow Mona,
so named because her moo was like a moan.
Savor the best grapes first, Butler means,
so there will be none better on the bunch,
and each will seem delicious to the last.
In truth, I don't quite follow the logic,
though his conclusion—past fifty,
everyone eats their days downward—
is unassailable.

What else?
That people who can whistle their speech.
My terminal confusion of *preterite* and *predicate*.
The meanings we live but do not have.
Oh, and Mona, who seemed less cow
than concept, really, half animal, half irony,
sticking her rubbable muzzle
through the fence like a Labrador.
We stayed a long while petting the impossibility of her.
We gave her—if you can believe it—grapes
left over from one daughter's lunch,
and when they were gone, and we were almost,

her moo blued the air like a sorrow
so absurd it left nothing left of us
but laughter.

WHATEVER THE BIRDS WERE

Like a spirited theological colloquy between two people
whose faith has failed,

two trees, alders, thrashed drastic in the gust
that subsided so suddenly it seemed each had inhaled, and stilled.

Whatever the birds were that flitted back and forth between them
then,
they made a silver-seeming noise.

FRAGMENT OF A LOST SCRIPTURE

Like an acolyte of earthquake, his laugh,
all quaff and rollick stomping down the dawn,
to stand a heron hour devouring clouds . . .
You knew no hunger till you'd tasted his.
Every adamant, even the utmost bone
of lean and gristled misery, split its richness:
the minnowing instants schooled to his whim;
to the tickle intelligence of godly philosophers
he proffered the feather of himself.
Such sweet soot and delicate battlements,
his hint of loot and ferment: earth
the element that he was, and worked, and dervished.
But was it *real*, satiety inevitably asked,
as a blood sun slipped from existence like a sigh:
our bog-rot nutmeat red roar of a savior,
bladdering past the licit trickles,
delivering precepts to the hurricane.

My friend's father is forgetting the world
but he remembers sex.
He will reach right out and caress the breast of a nurse.
And one day instead of toast he demands cunt
and forever after, that is what he smacks for breakfast.

I for whom God is not entirely gone am moved to wonder again
at the relation between chemistry and consciousness.
This belated tomcat candor, this crazed venereal rage,
was it, I wonder, during all those decades as a happy Catholic,
Little-League baseball coach, hedge-clipping citizen, loving
    husband, repressed?
Or was there a short as in a storm the fuse box flashes sharply
and all the windows but one go dark?
Is my friend's father's mind divided like a cocktail,
one part grace and two parts loss, with a splash of wrath?
God the tears as his granddaughter toddles happily toward his bed
and Beelzebub the buttered cunt?

My friend doesn't worry about this aspect of things.
He was close to his father and is trying to find some way
of being close to the void his father has become.
To the days that are, my friend says,
as we clink our drinks—whiskey, neat—and feel,
each in his own way, the tiny, divine starburst in the brain
by the gray, gray lake.

GIFT

Like a man who cannot bring himself to read the rules
for some elaborate contraption no one even needs,
screwing, banging, groping, grappling, fussing, forcing,
as if this glitch weren't latent in the very nature of things,
as if his own soul weren't arrested in the word *awry*,
as if the final goal were not to make but to emit
what all of time has never triggered: the perfect curse.

ALL MY FRIENDS ARE FINDING NEW BELIEFS

All my friends are finding new beliefs.
This one converts to Catholicism and this one to trees.
In a highly literary and hitherto religiously indifferent Jew
God whomps on like a genetic generator.
Paleo, Keto, Zone, South Beach, Bourbon.
Exercise regimens so extreme she merges with machine.
One man marries a woman twenty years younger
and twice in one brunch uses the word *verdant*;
another's brick-fisted belligerence gentles
into dementia, and one, after a decade of finical feints and teases
like a sandpiper at the edge of the sea,
decides to die.
Priesthoods and beasthoods, sombers and glees,
high-styled renunciations and avocations of dirt,
sobrieties, satieties, pilgrimages to the very bowels of being . . .
All my friends are finding new beliefs
and I am finding it harder and harder to keep track
of the new gods and the new loves,
and the old gods and the old loves,
and the days have daggers, and the mirrors motives,
and the planet's turning faster and faster in the blackness,
and my nights, and my doubts, and my friends,
my beautiful, credible friends.

ONE LOVE

1. *Sundays at Smilow*

Sundays are best.
The chemo drips
through the plastic tube
into the port implanted in my chest

and it is quiet, finally,
no one weeping
beyond the meaningless screens,
no one keeping

watch for a doctor
to tell them what one more
meaningless blood test means,
no swine of a man

emboldened by doom
grunting urges
to nurses,
no nurses consumed

with regularity or Ensure
or code-redding toward
someone's spastic reactions
to their cure.

No cure.
The chemo drips
through the plastic tube
into the port implanted in my chest.

Sundays are best.

2. A Dusk

How slowly the mountain
takes it in,
like a diagnosis
of darkness.

The consolation
of a continuation
that has nothing to do
with you.

3. *All You Shining Stars*

Three kinds of hair in the brush one love
has left on the kitchen counter.
Four kinds of cries when it occurs as one
to blow off school and go to the mountains.
And later, over the river, when the upturned duck
never turns over, five kinds of silence.

Always our elsewheres are also here,
like tributaries so intuitive they seem
almost incidentally literal, tiny trickles
in wildernesses too immense to enter,
the cold clefts and the drastic drops,
cliffs of unthinkable ice.

Three kinds of sleep in the hum home
down the dark valley back to New Haven.
Four kinds of dreams behind the headlights,
the world springing into being ten feet at a time.
Five kinds of time when one love wakes up
and wonders where we are, and one wonder
wakes up another, and another, and another.

BALONEY

Poolside, Belgian beer, the lightly ironized light
and splashy laughter of our perfect suburban summer
when from the water, from a child, comes something like
"Look alive, butt crack!"
"It was either that," Matt says, "or a whippoorwill."

Over shrimp and coconut rice that Annie made
I recall my dear donnish friend John
who asked that I please not "entertain company" in his bed.
And Samir, who also survived those years on beans, vagabondage,
and long letters that glittered with hopes and Helens,
wondered if I replied, "Will self-pleasure be ok?"

Spam sandwiches are something.
Then there's the Michigan Special John loved
(mayonnaise, peanut butter, and butter
mashed and slathered on fried white bread).
Mira says all she wanted from life once was baloney
and her mom, desperate at the deli counter, hissed,
"They make that out of dead people."

Such nuts we once knew! Whatever happened
to Helen anyway, the real one, whose over-ripe refinement
and parboiled moral sense demanded
a) evangelical veganism from the age of five;
b) that she end that vast chastity with a bang, as it were;
c) a chicken (Golden Polish), named (Gisuelda), tamed (it liked Rice
    Krispies) and given the run of the flat;
d) the alignment of Venus and Virgo;

e) a ring of candles on the floor; and, alas,
f) scissors.
"Gisuelda, it seems, did not share Helen's sense of ceremony."

Such laughter! Which makes us think of Elizabeth,
who wants her funeral to be a banquet
of which she herself is chief repast; and Zeke,
who fed his earlobes to nettled geckoes
and then appalled parties with his angry earrings;
and Don, buried barefoot and in his peace T-shirt
("This is the best letter I have ever received!
Well, no it's not, but you know what I mean.");
and Whitney, Craig, Martha, Tom.

"Four seconds," Annie says, bringing the blade
cleanly through the crimson watermelon.
"That's when a silence becomes officially awkward."
Drop-offs! The worst, everyone agrees.
Alex says sometimes she finds herself effusively praising
the very thing that's struck her dumb (if only!) with distaste.
Such sweetness. We let it run right down our mouths.

LAND'S END

for Nate Klug

I must have seen it seems a life of times
the same gray tanker like a nickel brick
stalled on the stark immaculate and thought
what chromosomal quicksands and cosmic squander,
what slime desire and shanty violence,
what filthy infant fist of original zilch,
and the cacti dialects, rum-sludge gazes landward,
dream seeps, night shouts, happiness hardy as a louse!
must lie behind and in that iron integument
mute and immured as any one man's heart.

DOING LINES AT THE COCKTAIL PARTY

October and even the air's professorial,
the day's deathlecture droning down in gray.

Pleasure, too, has its puritans,
its fanged savorings:

no meal so mediocre
that she'd allow some comfort in shared complaint.

—oh him and his puny glooms:
the dainties a dancer needs for nakedness to even be a thing.

Some intimate distance in the not-quite-light,
bombed-out small talk, skeletal chuckles:

two people grappling with the memory
of having grappled.

A coolness through which one nevertheless sweats,
like a friendship distance has thinned.

Even his praise was tainted with appraisal.
That smile invited and indicted you:
the whole of him a hole in him.

A sadness blaster, she said she was, scouring the house
with a kind of sexual psychic pesticide—

not altogether unavailing, I have to say.

  . . . something about him at once so consolingly formal
and devastatingly irrelevant, like a mortuary fern . . .

That air of creepy connoisseurship about him.
I felt as if I'd been sipped and set back down
by one who needed a moment to name the vintage.

I, too, annihilated all the little envies.
I, too, intuited the glorious swell

of Lady Marbury's marberries—
and looked away.

Capacity for happiness. My ex actually said that to me.
He'd discovered in himself a capacity for happiness.

It was as if some immense idiocy
had come to complete fruition in him,

like the century plant
that once a lifetime flowers and fouls the air

with its ironic resplendence,
its stalk of skunk.

•

The sad panache and fluent gloom of the golden boy gone old.

•

And her, the earth of her, all salt and tang, you could serve her on
    ice.

GOOD LORD THE LIGHT

Good morning misery,
goodbye belief,
good Lord the light
cutting across the lake
so long gone
to ice—

There is an under, always,
through which things still move, breathe,
and have their being,
quick coals and crimsons
no one need see
to see.

Good night knowledge,
goodbye beyond,
good God the winter
one must wander
one's own soul
to be.

POEM ENDING WITH A SENTENCE FROM JACQUES MARITAIN

It was the flash of black among the yellow billion.
It was the green chink on the chapel's sphere.
It was some rust or recalcitrance in us
by which we were by the grace of pain more here.
It was you, me, fall and fallen light.
It was that kind of imperfection
through which infinity wounds the finite.

I DON'T WANT TO BE A SPICE STORE

I don't want to be a spice store.
I don't want to carry handcrafted Marseille soap,
or tsampa and yak butter,
or nine thousand varieties of wine.
Half the shops here don't open till noon
and even the bookstore's brined in charm.
I want to be the one store that's open all night
and has nothing but necessities.
Something to get a fire going
and something to put one out.
A place where things stay frozen
and a place where they are sweet.
I want to hold within myself the possibility
of plugging one's ears and easing one's eyes;
superglue for ruptures that are,
one would have thought, irreparable,
a whole bevy of nontoxic solutions
for everyday disasters. I want to wait
brightly lit and with the patience
I never had as a child
for my father to find me open
on Christmas morning in his last-ditch, lone-wolf drive
for gifts. "Light of the World" penlight,
bobblehead compass, fuzzy dice.
I want to hum just a little with my own emptiness
at 4 a.m. To have little bells above my door.
To have a door.

II

WATERMELON HEAVEN

for Anne Halsey and Jeffrey Helgeson

The female fireman Doll
plops lobsters on plates
like little Brutalist buildings
made of rage.

Meat-headed, meat-handed, meat-eating men
so drunk their eyes
look uncircumcised.
Everywhere insides

are outside.
Iced oysters like tiny dirty nebulae.
A bag of gasping clams.
A boy whets a knife

to shuck a whelk
to show a girl a body
mostly foot. Eons of evolution to arrive
at this?

Here is bread, beer, beans, slaw.
A man wants something else.
Here's a line of port-a-potties
(perfected confessionals)

before which a line of pissers
only seems to lengthen,
a red bouncy castle bounces manically
like a house fire

seen through pain pills,
ten diminutive mutants trickle
loud and outlandish
out of the face-painting tent.

There is one end for everyone.
Short, taut, mute,
with that particular crinkled leanness that screams
nicotine, he raises a blade

almost as big as he is
and, as if a man could vanish
into what he did
if what he did were done for nothing

but the O on some stoner's mouth
or the little rockfall of applause
like the last soft *tocks*
of the avalanche,

samurais the air to a blur
of blade and red
and green and gone
that goes on, and on, and on.

A McDONALD'S IN MIDDLE AMERICA

Never again a nose like this
will I among the living witness;
nor the bulldog's little orchid anus
as it goes among the Winnebagos
and parked Harleys sniffing piss
like a vintner; nor the chalk
shocks and plaid slabs
of all the topological atrocities
slathered in booths;
nor erstwhile puerile truths
rising off the highway mind
like roadkill becoming its smell:
Absolutely unmixed attention
is prayer. Hell
is the inability to love.
Forever is composed of nows.
Never again.
Fifteen, sixteen maybe, and ensouled,
no doubt, as any of us,
but to all of us all proboscis,
he orders, pays, and waits
among us with the same
unseeing acuity of great beauty, or fame,
while we gobble our awe,
and feel for him,
and ponder the many ways of grace
for which we've been, till now, remiss.
Or am I alone in this?

THE SOUND

A bird sanctuary with no birds.
Eerie the beauty of the empty marsh.
No people even, soft apocalypse
of cordgrass, eelgrass, salt marsh pink,
the first sun refined and rebuffed by the Sound.
It became a game not to make a noise,
to let thoughts live or die in the eyes,
to entice wildness by the pure force of our peace.
Shells went uncrushed, twigs missed, words averted flesh . . .
There was a hint of something then,
almost a call, but so thin it seemed a memory
even as it happened, too vague to name, impossible to follow.
Some part of us remains.
Some part of us pauses still on that path,
with the unpiping piping plover, and the invisible bittern,
and the once common knot.

TWO DRINKING SONGS

1. *Up with a Twist*

The scriptural mentions of martinis were,
he allowed, scant, and The Thin Place
a diabolically ironic name for a bar,

yet one feels a certain spiritual imperative,
as it were, from the earth, as it were,
a call to a clarity one can taste and see,

wine, that unctuous embodied smell,
being but water and a touch of luck
to butter the liver of a Christian.

2. *Neat*

Six sharp,
whiskey's instant,
little sulfur savor
in the brain,

pain by no means
in abeyance
but the will and wherewithal
to see it

sip by sip
diminishing,
the whole of it all
misting mercifully over

like a peak
Li Po might have looked
free of meaning
on the cold road to Shu.

TEN DISTILLATIONS

Apophatic
He talked of nothingness until it wasn't.
He bragged his gravity into God.

Convert
What did he learn when he learned of his own bad heart?
That scared and sacred are but a beat apart.

Skeptic
His eyes were open but his heart was shut.
At the edge of every wonder he said *But* . . .

Inspiration
"The clearest morning is a thing to bear,"
he writes, overjoyed, once more, by despair.

Knowledge
To touch the summit was to learn so much.
Among which: there are summits you can't touch.

Via Negativa
He names his love by naming what he hates.
Joy generalizes. Pain individuates.

Near Death
Not beyond, but beyond my power to tell.
What Eden sweeter than the one in hell?

Apophatic
Why wouldn't I praise the vacuous black?
The one abundance I could trust was lack.

Natural Theology
Dawn, light dew on the grass, the air cool, clear.
Nothing more. Nothing mere.

The End of Prayer
    —that I might cry life
like any bird belonging to its dawn.

A HERESY

Once after a lecture a woman stood up and read a passage out of
some prose I had written and said, "How do you feel about being
a heretic?" What I should have answered is that there are no
heretics, or that there are only heretics; that humans—mere and
mirrored creatures that we are—move toward God in language,
and to speak language is to profane him. I should have said that I
grew up in a land God held in the very palm of his hand, lifting
us all up lovingly to the light, breathing over us his tender winds,
and then, almost as an afterthought, periodically crushing it all
to dust. I should have said how does one praise a God in whom
one does not believe, and how does one believe in a God whose
only evidence of existence is one's insatiable and perhaps insane
desire to praise? I should have said that "no human being possesses
sureness of self: this can only mean being bounded and unbounded,
selved and unselved, 'sure' only of this untiring exercise. Then, this
sureness of self, which is ready to be unsure, makes the laughter at
the mismatch between aim and achievement comic, not cynical;
holy, not demonic. This is not love of suffering, but the work, the
power of love, which may curse, but abides. It is power to be able *to
attend*, powerful or powerless; it is love to laugh bitterly, purgatively,
purgatorially, and then to be quiet."

ASSEMBLY

It may be Lord our voice is suited now
only for irony, onslaught, and the minor hierarchies of rage.

It may be only the crudest, cruelest transformations touch us,
gauzewalkers in the hallways of a burn ward.

I remember a blind man miraculous for the sounds of his mouth,
every bird rehearsed and released for the children to cheer.

Where is he now, in what icy facility or sunlit square,
blackout shades and a brambled mouth, singing extinctions?

AND SOMEONE WROTE IT DOWN

I read about a bomber whose favorite fruit was dates.
Somewhere, in the annihilating light and the no-time-to-cries,
amid the sudden silica of the market stalls,
the whirlwinded bones and the misted viscera: dates.
A brother said he'd loved them. Said it, I imagine,
with the same lonely catatonia of the saint
when God withdraws, and then withdraws His withdrawal,
until there's nothing but a word for what had been a world.
Someone picked up the pieces. Someone scrubbed the blood.
Someone clung to something human, and someone wrote it down.

THE PRIEST AT THE POOL PARTY

Bound with vows
like Ulysses strapped to the mast,
he drifts past
the white sirens of their thighs,

the scooped fruits and toothpicked meats
displayed on the table,
and is almost able
to taste the love a lack completes.

A SKETCH

An air of old hotel about him: bitters and rye,
pornographers in penguin suits, glaucous Dover sole.

Derringer words—*doff, peruse*—
which he hardly needs to use, to use.

Morals as involved as baklava.
He brushes crumbs from his lapel as if he had one.

Death? Who knew the rube's recessive treasures
better than he, who knew himself?

So he folded, a paragon of suave
aced at the end by galumphing luck.

DEATH WILL HAVE TO BE CAREFUL HERE

My friend in whose eyes I realize
there has never been rest
says Fairfield Porter's interiors
don't hold us hostage to their moods,
vermouth *insipids* vodka,
and of all the bright criers Puck is best.
Death will have to be careful here,
I think, as, deep in a wilderness,
in a time so dry that time itself is tinder,
a man kicks dust over every last ash
of last night's fire, and still,
four hills and a river later,
pauses in a panic. "The might
to move what her eye fell upon
is the image of her I keep,
her iridescent readiness."

HOW FUN WHEN YOUNG

How fun when young to feel your death
browsing around you like a little goat.
It bleats, it gambols, it eats
your undies right off the line if you let it.
So you do, you do.

How easesome to eat some
chilaquiles and churros of a Sunday,
little prinks and glints of eyes and ice,
hours and orifices just waiting for your will to fill them.
So you do, you do.

Comes now the night
over all the suburb's impervious surfaces
and thirsty lawns, all the tiny alliances
of line and shadow, hush and wish.
So you do.

SOMETHING OF THE SKY

A pilot towered into our house
his shirt white as a shout
something of the sky still clinging to him.
The children passed his hat between them like a crown.

Later—chatty, khaki,
tropical chocolates and foreign coins
spilling out of his pockets—
it was as if upstairs he'd stored a roar.

All weekend I could almost hear it.
All weekend I felt a hum
inside the furniture, and prayed,
if you could call that panic prayer.

He was up at dawn—
all glint and epaulette, crease and gleam,
as if his very being had been ironed—
and gone.

Too tall for the taxi, he bent his hinges
into the backseat
and gave the wave all givers give
for whom a stay is brief and between is home.

MILD DRY LINES: AN EXCHANGE

       —You prick too liberal into alien pains,
and read too readily a grief you need to see
in order for the world to be the world
that ratifies the choices you've made.
You talk of callings, but a calling should
enlarge the life that it refines,
not grind its spice into some same mustard.

       —If we could see the grief of any one life
it would be slag enough to crust a world
and any feeling being buried within.
But grief's a craft like any other, it seems,
if only indirectly ours:
our skin's inscripted with what nature knows.
The dead child chiseled in that woman's cheek,
the battle smoldering off that old man's brow,
our very mirrors, friend, these aging faces
with their lines of loneliness like pressured ice:
you would have them silenced?

                              —I would have them whole.

       —As would I. As would anyone
whose life is lit, however dimly, by the light
of survival.

       —I fear that by survival what you mean
is resignation, or, worse, a fictioned oblivion,
like the bull elephant that has outgrown

the stake that it was tied to as a calf:
it cannot break the rope that it could break
with ease.

       —And I fear by wholeness what you mean
is merely the will to leaven fate with will,
that constipated sorrow called good cheer.
I won't relapse from these mild dry lines
whose only consolation is their dryness,
that one might utter calmly utter blood.

AH, EGO

Ah, ego,
my beetle,
my cockroach

crawling out of the holocaust
of lost keys, bad screws,
and what have you,

how little singed you are,
how almost spry,
tentacling intact

past the wrecks and drecks
and what have you,
moon rover roving over

the moon of me . . .

III

THE PARABLE OF PERFECT SILENCE

Today I woke and believed in nothing.
A grief at once intimate and unfelt,
like the death of a good friend's dog.

Tired of the mind reaching back in the past for rescue
I praise the day.
I don't mean merely some mythical, isolate instant
like the mindless mindfulness specialist
who at the terminal cancer convention
(not that it was called that)
exhorted the new year's crop of slaughters
(ditto)
to "taste" the day, this one unreplicable instant of being alive.
(The chicken glistened.)
Nor do I mean a day devoid of past and future
as craved that great craze of minds and times Fernando Pessoa,
who wanted not "the present" but reality itself,
things in their thingness rather than the time that measures them.
Time is in the table at which I sit and in the words I type.
In the red-checked shirt my father's mother used to wear
when she was gardening and which I kept
because it held her smell (though it does no longer)
there is still plenty of time.

Two murderers keep their minds alive
while they wait to die.
They talk through slots in their doors
of whatever mercy or misery
the magazine has ordained for the day—
the resurgence of the Taliban in Afghanistan, say,
ten signs that a relationship is on the rocks.
When their communion flags, as communions will,
they rekindle it with personal revelations, philosophical digressions,
humor. This is a true story,
one of them says sometimes by way of preface,
as if that gives the moment more gravity,
asks of the listener a different attention,
at once resists and reinforces an order
wherein every hour has its sound, every day its grace,
and every death is by design.

"Love is possible for anyone," I hear the TV talk-show host say,
which is true in the way most things in this life are true,
which is to say, false,
unless and until the nullifying, catalyzing death is felt.
Love is possible for anyone
because it is equally impossible for everyone.
To be is to be confronted with a void,
a blankness, a blackness that both appeals and appalls.
Once known—known by the void, I mean—one has three choices.
Walk away, and unlearn the instinct of awe.

Walk along, and learn to believe that awe asks nothing of you.
Are you with me, love?

(For love read faith.)

Naked once and after a rat my father cried "Die, vermin, die!"
banging the broomstick over and over on the floor
so incorrigibly dirty it might as well have been the earth itself.
This is my mother's story, though I was there, I'm told,
and no small part of the pandemonium.
We were five souls crammed into one life,
and so incorrigibly poor—or was that fear?—we all slept in one
        room
and shared one great big chester drawers, as we called it,
and not with irony but in earnest ignorance,
just as *like* meant *lack*, as in
"How much do you like bein' done with your chemo?"
and just as I and every other child I knew,
before we tucked into our lemon meringue pie,
solemnly wiped the calf slobbers off.
Ah, local color, peasant levity, the language fuming and steaming
rich as the mist of rot that rises off the compost heap
("kitchen midden," you might hear an old Scot still say).
When do we first know? That there's a world
to which we've been, not oblivious, exactly,

but so inside we couldn't see it, who now see nothing else?
Heaven is over. Or hell.
Did you forget the rat?
It thumps and thrashes like a poltergeist inside
the chest of drawers but somehow, though my father is fast,
and though his rage is becoming real, every drawer he opens
is empty. What happens when we die,
every child of every father eventually asks.
What happens when we don't
is the better question.

To kill a wasp on water is the peak of speed.
My brother who is other has a mind of lead.
I with my stinging griefs watch from away.
How can it be there are no adults left?
What matters here is timing, not time.
His hand is high and white above the blue.
A wasp is also atom and urge, hover and touch.
Even wings are not a clean distinction.
Down comes the slap like a rifle shot.
What vengeance can there be on blank necessity?
My brother who is other has a way.
His hand is high and white. And then it's not.

Once when my father's mother's health was failing
and she found it more and more difficult to tend
to the tiny family plot in Champion, Texas,
which is less town than time at this point,
a blink of old buildings and older longings the rare driver
flashes past, I took it upon myself to salt the graves
as I must have read somewhere would work for unwanted growths.
As indeed it did.
In the months after, every Sunday when we spoke,
she thanked me for the blankness, the blackness,
(my words, of course)
this new ease I had allowed her mind.
Until one day leaning over with flowers the leached earth
opened and my eighty-year-old grandmother
tumbled right down among the bones
of the woman from whom she'd first emerged.
To see that image you have to be that sky.
It has to happen in you, that crushing, calling viewless blue
so deeply in you that it is not you.
"O, Law', honey, I like to died."

You don't climb out of poverty so much as carry it with you.
Some shell themselves with wealth.
Some get and spend, get and spend, skimming existence like a
    Jesus lizard.
But for those whose souls have known true want
—whose souls perhaps *are* true want—

money remains, in some sense, permanently inert,
like an erotic thought that flashes through a eunuch's brain.
In 1980 my father bought his first airplane,
a scream-proof four-seater we crammed five inside,
which he considerately slammed into a sorghum field alone.
Unkillable, he killed ten years with work and wives,
then bought another, and brought it down in the solitary fire
that was his aspect and atmosphere. Homes, schemes,
thirty years of savings plowed into a sign company (!)
that did not, it turned out, exist.
A hole is hard to carry.

People ask if I believe in God and the verb is tedious to me.
Not wrong, not offensive, not intrusive, not embarrassing.
Tedious.
Today I saw a hawk land on Elizabeth's chimney.
It sat with its bone frown and banker's breast
above the proud houses of Hamden.
Are you with me? Then see,
too, a lump of animate ash rising from the flue
(or so it seems) to be a pigeon
fluttering dumbly down
next to that implacable raptor,
suddening a world of strange relations
wherein there is no need for fear, or far,
or meat.

There was a man made of airplane parts,
one of which was always missing.
He wandered the hospital grounds in search of a rudder,
an aileron, or some other fragment
that would let him fly from this place
where he was not meant to be.
There was a woman who emitted invective
ceaselessly, dispassionately, an obscenity machine.
One soul saved Saran Wrap for five full years
and every night wrought it into an ever more solid ball
with which, it turned out, he planned to bash the skull
of the first person he saw the dawn God blessed his weapon.
(A success story, alas.)
Another man with anvil hands sat six months of nights in faith
that there would come occasion of darkness, unguardedness, and
    vision
sufficient to rip from its socket one of my father's bright blue eyes.
(Ditto.)
My father moved among them like a father.
He attended and pacified, he instructed and consoled.
Late to the trade, he worked too much,
and trusted his heart, no doubt, more than he should,
but was, by all accounts, at this one thing, and despite the end,
    good.

For love read faith
into these lines that so obviously lack it.

For love let words turn to life
in the way life turns to world
under the observer's eye, the swirl
of particles with their waves and entanglements,
their chance and havoc, resolving
into some one thing:
a raptor on a rooftop, say.
No power on earth can make it stay.
But is it lost or released into formlessness
when we look away?

To be is to believe
that the man or woman
who inscribed with an idiosyncratic but demanding calligraphy
Fuck da money—Trust no one
on the rough blanket of the residential motel
where my father spent the last two years of his rough residential life
intended the note of defiant, self-conscious (*da!*) humor
that left my father, whom I had not seen in years,
and I, whom years had seen grow sere, far even from myself,
erupting in laughter until we cried.

Before my good friend's good dog died
ten times a day she pressed her forehead to his
to confirm the world and her place in it.

Now she won't even say his name.
Strange how the things that burn worst in one heart
one must keep silent to keep.

Ten to one you thought of men.
The murderers, I mean.
But no. This is a true story.
There is another cell, you see,
in which a woman I have known since childhood,
and since childhood have known to be
suspended on a wire of time but nimble-witted nonetheless,
lies on the cold stone floor.
She is even more naked than they have made her.
She has killed no one not even herself.
It is punishment, perhaps, or some contagion of fate,
her hair shorn, both wrists wrapped, eyes open,
pondering the parable of perfect silence.

Remember, he said, *memory is a poor man's prison.*
Make to have and to love one live infinitive,
then blessed my brow with the sign of the cross.
I woke without a chance to ask the obvious:
But what if all our songs are songs of loss?

I felt nothing when you died, Father.
(As if I ever called you that.)
It is a long cold seep, this grief.
The day itself was hot enough to make the devil sweat,
as more than one person, with less than one mind, muttered to me.
What I remember: two children, too tan
and "clad in famine" (Dahlberg), look up
from their parched front yard,
their sad little sprinkler like a flower of hell.
I don't mean I saw them, though I did.
I mean they are *what I remember*, fleshed.
That town. A hint of new prison business,
and the Square's been rewhitened,
but mostly it's beastly, a blast site,
our old house less house than nest,
and even the undertaker, a friend
from high school, has graduated to heroin.
You would have been right at home,
and I guess in a ghoulish way you were,
overdressed, overdosed, over.
Hard wind at the graveside. Hard lives hardly there.
The canopy whipped and flapped.
A bouquet skipped over the graves like a strange elation.
Something stuck, and an ageless Indian
(he might have been Mom's long-dead granddad)
nimbled over the casket's contraptions to make it go. You go
into the ground again, and the silence assaults
like heat, and the clumps of would-be grievers unclump
and head for cars, and Mom cracks

a tall boy and two jokes before we're on the highway.
The first I forget, and of the second I recall only a nakedness, and
    wild crying,
and a rat.

When the doctor said I'd likely die I thought of my father
telling me he'd learned to read a cancer look,
that some people had it before they had it, so to speak.
When the young guard demanded to unwrap the Snickers
I'd bought for my sister my father scoffed:
"All this energy expended on candy when you could take this can"
—he held her Coke up in front of our eyes—"and cut a throat."
When my sister, chewing her chocolate with ravenous indifference,
paused and stared balefully off at the even more baleful brown
beyond the barbed wire, it did not occur to me
that it was inspiration. When I began writing these lines
it was not, to be sure, inspiration but desperation,
to be alive, to believe again in the love of God.
The love of God is not a thing one comprehends
but that by which—and only by which—one is comprehended.
It is like the child's time of pre-reflective being,
and like that time, we learn it by its lack.
Flashes and fragments, flashes and fragments,
these images are not facets of some unknowable whole
but entire existences in themselves, like worlds
that under God's gaze shear and shear and, impossibly, are:
untouching, entangled, sustained, free.

If all love demands imagination, all love demands withdrawal.
We must create the life creating us, and must allow that life to be.
And to be beyond, perhaps, whatever we might imagine.
I, too, am more (and less)
than anything I imagine myself to be.
"To know this," says Simone Weil, "is forgiveness."

It is an air you enter, not an act you make.
It is the will's frustration, and is the will's fruition.
It is to wade a blaze one night that I once crossed
—a young man, and lost—
to find a woman made of weather
sweeping the street in front of her shack.
It is another country.
It is a language I don't know.
La por allá, la por allá, I repeat in my sleep.
The over there.

Tired of the mind reaching back in the past for rescue
I praise the day
my father woke in the motel room where all of us were sleeping,
which is not even past but a flame as I say it,
and see it, the little lighter now he is using to find his clothes.
I who have not slept in forty-five years am awake for the first time
rising carefully out of my pallet on the floor

and feeling my way beyond the bodies of my brother and sister
toward the shade that is my father
to stand in this implausible light where to whisper would be too
    much,
and anyway what's next is known, Dad, and near,
the nowhere diner, hot chocolate and the funny pages,
and the consolation that comes when there is nothing to console.

IV

• • •

FIFTY

"Renouncing kingship like a snot of phlegm"
I go out into the park. I have my death with me,
iron friend, and a few feather regrets
that one by one lift from me in the wind.
I have two daughters and one cloud, an old oak
and a great love, elected solitude, given sun.
There never was a now this golden one.

EVEN BEES KNOW WHAT ZERO IS

That's enough memories, thank you, I'm stuffed.
I'll need a memory vomitorium if this goes on.
How much attention can one man have?
Which reminds me: once I let the gas go on flowing
after my car was full and watched it spill its smell
(and potential hell) all over the ground around me.
I had to pay for that, and in currency quite other than attention.
I've had my fill of truth, too, come to think of it.
It's all smeary in me, I'm like a waterlogged Bible:
enough with the aborted prophecies and garbled laws,
ancient texts holey as a teen's jeans, begone begats!
Live long enough, and you can't tell what's resignation, what resolve.
That's the bad news. The good news? You don't give a shit.
My life. It's like a library that closes for a long, long time
—a *lifetime*, some of the disgrunts mutter—
and when it opens opens only to an improved confusion:
theology where poetry should be, psychology crammed with math.
And I'm all the regulars searching for their sections
and I'm the detonated disciplines too.
But most of all I'm the squat, smocked, bingo-winged woman
growing more granitic and less placable by the hour
as citizen after citizen blurts some version of
"What the hell!" or "I thought you'd all died!"
and the little stamp she stamps on the flyleaf
to tell you when your next generic mystery is due
that thing goes *stamp* right on my very soul.
Which is one more thing I'm done with, by the way,
the whole concept of soul. Even bees know what zero is,
scientists have learned, which means bees know my soul.

I'm done, I tell you, I'm due, I'm Oblivion's datebook.
I'm a sunburned earthworm, a mongoose's milk tooth,
a pleasure tariff, yesterday's headcheese, spiritual gristle.
I'm the Apocalypse's Popsicle. I'm a licked Christian.

FACULTY MEETING, DIVINITY SCHOOL

First Thursday, 3:59,
  before the beard,
    behind which

the Dean's demeanor is,
  like the ocean,
    so open

it isn't, calls on the tall
  philosopher, who alone believes
    in heaven, to pray—

and the destruction
  of the old chapel
    passes,

Grief and Dying
  is no longer
    an elective,

and a Chair raises a question
  no one is equipped
    to answer—

the pretty balletic
  scholar of Paul
    leans like a heron

over last month's minutes.

RACCOON PROBLEM

Like an exasperation of starlings.

Like a mountain climber who on his way up
passes the bones of those who died trying.

Like Hittite sexual ethics,
for whom relief in a sheep was acceptable,
but if you fucked a donkey, you were done.

Like a man who tucked his deepest truth in rhyme
so no one would ever find it, or only the right no ones.

Like scholars in a formal reading room who, passing hours
poring through the delicate pages of the dead, look up,
meet each other's eyes with a slight nod and tight smile,
then drop back into their separate centuries.

Like the Alp alto of the shy child,
who sings completely only when facing away.

Like the ox-eye daisy that is anything but,
the creek-side cow path and the vernacular water,
the sun sunning, the birds birding, the mind.

Like a laconic grandpa with (or rather without) a raccoon problem:
"I dispatched him with a shovel and threw him in the trash."

Another morning of mist.
How many do I have left?
Another morning of missed.
The habit of lack is hell
to break. The German girl
had a little black abyss
between her two front teeth
that flashed—if you can imagine
blackness flashing—through everything
she said. She said,
pinning back her turbulent hair
and cheerfully chewing English
like a *Sonnenblumenbrot*,
that she was "tensed"
about the poetry in my class,
since it comes—the little abyss!—
from the, how do you say,
"breath-crystal" of a language?
There had been for both of us
a boy—American, obviously,
and Midwestern, I would guess—
who raised his hand like a clean
stalk of wheat and asked
in a way that was already an answer,
Shouldn't an experience of God
bring us, I don't know, peace?
It rained while I was writing this.
It rained, and my father died,
and it stopped, and it rained,

and I leaned down close to a flower
for which I had no name, and it stopped,
and my great-great-granddaughter
tried to think what it might mean
to pray and it rained
and it burned and I found myself
in front of faces talking less
about connections than the seams
between things because it seems
no matter the knowledge or vision
there is this need, this void, this
mist. "The poem is lonely,"
the poet says. "It intends another
and it goes out toward her."
You come downstairs
wearing what you wear
and moving as you move
up to the glass beside me, where we see,
mostly, what we do not see:
neighbors and playthings, tree limbs
one tick past implicit.
Even the sun's in trust.

Avid the vastness to eat everything in sight:
bone mule, dun man, westward leastward grow the trees,
even the clouds irradiated into blue.
Here in cucumber Connecticut it reaches even me,
hard land, hard light that I without seeing see.
It would be a mercy not to name it God.
It would be assent and assertion both to stand,
human, in a final light feeling nothing
but light, as from the land, and from the mind,
it fades, and cedes to even greater space.
It would be nerve and star, nowhere, near.
It would be creeping and it would be teeth.
It would be darkness, darkness, darkness.
And it would come morning.

MAUNDERSONG

Sometimes it seems we're being used.
Rage no more one's own than heat in the desert stone:
the man stands baffled amid the blood of what he's done.
Or in the after-rapture, in the wreckage of their calls and smells,
the lovers meet each other eyes as if . . . meeting each other.
"You are in me deeper than I am in me,"
Augustine said, but that's not what I mean.
More a storm in which there is no you, no me, no in, and decidedly
    no out.
What was that weeping coming out of me at 3 a.m.?
O fireless lines, my little maundersong,
I know you are nothing. But you're mine.

It didn't matter, the muttering hordes,
her perpendicular intellect, his vinegar eloquence,
the black capital locked in ice like a verdict.
I woke, I was, naked as a hazelnut,
explicit and unencumbered as a pagan orgasm.
I felt so myself my sorrows were plumage.
I strode the word *boulevard*.

A LIGHT STORE IN THE BOWERY

Some love is like a light store
you slip inside only to escape
the rain. Something to see, it turns out:
the plasma lamps, mosque and lava,
the elegant icicles of the chandeliers,
shapes and shades so insistently singular
that rooms can't help but happen around them,
lives can't help but acquire choices and chances
inside. Some love is like an old owner
who when a child walks in with her parents
can only imagine shatterings.
And some love is like that child
asking with an earnest and exemplary awe,
"Where do they keep the dark?"

FLIGHT

In the end we love the line love cannot cross.
In the end we fall for what we fail.

Forget friendship. Ardor.
Forget the years that only grow harder

as the soul recedes in what the years bring,
grown alien to any touchable thing.

Touch me. As I am. As you can.
My heart a bird's heart just beyond your hand.

after Anna Akhmatova

NEVER HEAVEN

1.

Remember? Our faces still flushed
from the regions each in each had opened,
we stepped outside to find the time
had turned to snow:

soft approximate rooftops,
the parked car like a grounded cloud,
each particular tree limb, phone wire, fence post
more visible for having vanished.

2.

Do you remember
the hours' cashmere,

every pore aware,
novitiates of never?

It left us useless
for less.

AFTER A LECTURE WITH MY LOVE

Light, when it goes, goes everywhere at once.
The photon that hurtles toward Earth at 186,282 miles a second
flashes just as fast away.

But let a leaf, say, intrude, or a moon, or a man,
and what was everywhere and always is always only one,
and done.

To speak a thing one can't conceive.
To live in the instant before the instant is.
To feel infinities going dark for this one light along your thigh.

JOY

A jet's white track,
a radio's blare—

sunlight suddenly more itself
on the roofer's tool,

flashed back
into its everywhere.

EPILOGUE

The more I think the more I feel
reality without reverence is not real.

·

The more I feel the more I think
that God himself has brought me to this brink
wherein to have more faith means having less.
And love's the sacred name for loneliness.

·

I speak a word I have not spoken
and by that word am broken open,
a cry entirely other entirely mine.

·

In league with the stones of the field
I am by being healed.

NOTES

p. 37: The italicized lines are from Simone Weil, Fyodor Dostoevsky, and Emily Dickinson.

p. 41: "Joy generalizes. Pain individuates" is a quote from Johann Peter Hebel, which I first discovered in Anna Kamienska's notebooks (translated by Clare Cavanagh).

p. 43: The quotation is from Gillian Rose's *Love's Work*.

p. 48: The quoted lines are from W. S. Di Piero's poem "Moving Things."

p. 73: The first line is from the *Siksa Samuccaya: A Compendium of Buddhist Doctrine* (translated by Cecil Bendall and W. H. D. Rouse).

p. 78: "Meaning is not man's gift to reality" is a quote from Abraham Joshua Heschel. The quoted lines in this poem are from Paul Celan.

p. 80: "We pray God to be free of God" is a quote from Meister Eckhart.

ACKNOWLEDGMENTS

I am grateful to the editors of the following magazines and anthologies, where some of these poems first appeared: *America, The American Scholar, The Arkansas International,* the Best American Poetry series, *The Christian Century, Commonweal, The Hopkins Review, The New Yorker, The New York Review of Books, Plough Quarterly, Poetry, Poetry International, Rascal, The Sewanee Review, Spiritus, Subtropics, Terrain.org, The Yale ISM Review.*